*Other Simon Rose novels
you will enjoy*

THE ALCHEMIST'S PORTRAIT

THE SORCERER'S LETTERBOX

THE CLONE CONSPIRACY

THE EMERALD CURSE

THE HERETIC'S TOMB

THE DOOMSDAY MASK

D1483556

The Time Camera

SIMON ROSE

VANCOUVER   LONDON

Distribution and representation in Canada by
Fitzhenry & Whiteside • www.fitzhenry.ca

Distribution and representation in the UK by
Turnaround • www.turnaround-uk.com

Released in the USA in 2012

Mixed Sources
Cert no. SW-COC-001271
© 1996 FSC

FSC

Inside pages printed on FSC certified paper using vegetable-based inks.

Manufactured by Sunrise Printing
Manufactured in Chilliwack, BC, Canada in October 2011

2 4 6 8 10 9 7 5 3 1

Cataloguing-in-Publication Data for this book
is available from The British Library.

Library and Archives Canada Cataloguing in Publication

Rose, Simon, 1961-
The time camera / Simon Rose.

ISBN 978-1-896580-09-8

I. Title.

PS8585.O7335T54 2011   jC813'.6   C2011-905533-3

This book is dedicated to
the memory of Angela Mary Rose,
devoted wife, mother and grandmother
1934 to 2010

"Don't grieve for me, for now I'm free,
I'm following the path God laid for me,
I took his hand when I heard his call,
I turned my back and left it all."

Sadly missed

—S.R.

Tradewind Books thanks the Governments of Canada and British Columbia for
the financial support they have extended through the Canada Book Fund, Livres
Canada Books, the Canada Council for the Arts, the British Columbia Arts
Council and the British Columbia Book Publishing Tax Credit program.

**Canada Council
for the Arts**

**Conseil des Arts
du Canada**

BRITISH COLUMBIA
ARTS COUNCIL
Supported by the Province of British Columbia

LIVRES CANADA BOOKS

Contents

Prologue   Chamberlain Research   11

Chapter 1   Eleanor's Legacy   16

Chapter 2   Uncle Magnus   24

Chapter 3   Intruders   30

Chapter 4   Pictures of the Past   34

Chapter 5   A Dangerous Discovery   42

Chapter 6   Sinclair Enterprises   50

Chapter 7   Stealing Tomorrow   58

Chapter 8   Future Imperfect   65

Chapter 9   An Unwelcome Visitor   68

Chapter 10   Journey to Yesterday   74

Chapter 11   A Change of Course   78

Chapter 12   Twisting Time   84

Chapter 13   Reversal of Fortunes   88

Prologue

Chamberlain Research

Eleanor Chamberlain frantically deleted all the computer files and tossed any important research notes and documents into the garbage can, soaking them with chemicals from the lab and setting them alight. The fire spread quickly. She prayed that the smoke wouldn't trigger any alarms and regretfully watched as all her research turned into ashes.

All that remained was the camera itself.

As she studied the device, Eleanor marvelled that something so unassuming could possess such extraordinary power. The camera was an incredible discovery, but Eleanor knew that it was far too dangerous to fall into the wrong hands. She knew what she had to do.

All the designs and blueprints had been burned beyond recognition, and Eleanor prepared to drop the camera itself into the fire.

"What do you think you're doing?"

Eleanor spun around to see her research partner, Magnus Sinclair, standing in the doorway less than twenty feet away.

"I already told you, Magnus," Eleanor replied, maintaining a firm grip on the camera, "this project is too dangerous."

"What are you talking about?" he asked, edging toward her.

"You know what I mean, Magnus," she said sternly. "You said as much yourself."

"But think of the possibilities, Eleanor! We could both be rich beyond our wildest dreams. You know as well as I do, this isn't about the past. It's about the future. About the technology and all the inventions still to be discovered. It could all belong to us."

"It's still theft, no matter how you look at it."

"But no one would ever know," Magnus retorted. "How could they?"

"I can't allow it," insisted Eleanor, shaking her head. "I've already burned all the research notes and deleted all the computer files. We need to end this—right now."

She turned to drop the camera into the flames still burning in the garbage can, but Magnus lunged at her. In the struggle, Eleanor's elbow knocked over the chemicals by the computer, spilling them onto the fire, which erupted in a tower of flame.

In the confusion, Magnus grabbed the camera, seconds before an explosion ripped through the lab. When the smoke cleared, he could see Eleanor trapped under a heavy steel filing cabinet.

"Magnus!" she cried. "Magnus, help me, I can't move my legs!"

But he put the camera into his pocket and backed away toward the door.

"Magnus!" she screamed. "Don't leave me!"

Suddenly there was a second, larger explosion.

13

Magnus was thrown through the laboratory doorway and landed in the hallway. He struggled to his feet, stumbled into the shattered lobby and rushed outside to safety.

In the ambulance, a young paramedic dressed a wound on Magnus' left cheek. He had been cut close to his ear by a shard of flying glass. He instinctively moved his hand toward his face, but the paramedic stopped him.

"Don't touch that," she told him. "What happened in there?"

"I'm not sure," Magnus said. "There was an explosion. My colleague is trapped in there!"

The paramedic patted his shoulder. "They're doing all they can, but I'm afraid it doesn't look good. The firefighters told us not to expect anyone else coming out alive. I'm sorry about your friend."

"I tried to save her," Magnus said.

"You're lucky to be alive," the paramedic said. "You seem to be fine. You should be able to go home."

"Thanks," he said.

Magnus Sinclair stepped down from the ambulance and walked onto the lawn in front of the now hardly recognizable building. He watched the blaze as it continued to destroy what was left of Chamberlain Research.

Magnus felt the weight of the camera in his pocket. He smiled to himself. No one could survive an explosion like that. Not only was Eleanor sure to be dead, but all evidence that the camera had ever existed, along with all the other research into what they had called time photography, was now gone. There would be no trail for anyone to follow once he put his plans into action.

Chapter One

Eleanor's Legacy

Jake rang the doorbell at his friend Lydia's house. Her dad, Greg, opened the door.

"Hey, Jake," Greg said. "You just caught me. I've got to pick up a few things for lunch from the store. Lydia's uncle is coming over. She's upstairs."

Jake stepped through the entrance into the hallway.

"Lydia, Jake's here!" Greg yelled.

"Be right down!"

"Okay, Jake, got to run," said Greg. "Make yourself at home. See you later."

Jake wandered into the sitting room. While he waited for Lydia, he looked at the Chamberlain family photos on the mantelpiece. They showed Lydia and Greg on vacation in Disneyland, London, Hawaii and the Rockies. There was also an older photo of Lydia with her mom. Lydia's mother was a tall elegant woman with a long slender neck, blue eyes, a radiant smile and short wavy brown hair. Eleanor Chamberlain had died two years before in a fire at the research laboratory where she'd worked. There was also a picture of her taken at the laboratory, standing beside a man with thick black hair and pale grey eyes. Between them they held a brass plaque inscribed with the words CHAMBERLAIN RESEARCH.

Jake and his family had moved into the neighbourhood only about a year before, so he had never met Lydia's mother.

"Hey, Jake."

He turned around to see Lydia, who bore a strong resemblance to her mother. She was carrying something under her arm.

"Is that a new laptop?" asked Jake.

"New to me," Lydia replied. "It was my mom's. She used it for work. Dad just gave it to me. He found it at the back of one of the upstairs closets. The battery's dead, though, and the charger is in the basement office. I was just about to go down there."

Jake followed Lydia down to the basement. In the office there were a couple of computers, a desk and three filing cabinets. Lydia set her mother's old laptop down on the nearest filing cabinet. A layer of dust covered just about everything; the room had scarcely been touched since Eleanor had died.

"She used to call this her sanctuary, where she could get away and work when she was at home. In the last couple of months before the accident, Dad and I hardly saw her . . ." She trailed off.

"Are you okay?" Jake asked as he sat down in the chair and opened one of the desk drawers.

"Yeah," said Lydia, "I'm okay. Do you see the charger anywhere?"

"No," Jake replied. "Maybe she left it at the lab."

He closed the drawer, pushed the chair away from the desk and stood up. Turning, he tripped on the edge of a rug. He was about to smooth it out when something on the floor caught his eye.

"There's something down here," he said.

He stooped by the desk and pulled back the rug to reveal a wooden rectangle in the concrete floor, about the same size as a heating vent. Jake gently lifted the plank and saw that underneath was a recessed compartment. Inside, there was an object covered with a piece of cloth. Jake reached in and pulled it out, laid it next to the keyboard, then sat back down at the desk and removed the cloth.

"It's a camera," Lydia said.

"It's not a type I'm familiar with," Jake said.

Like any digital camera, it had a screen on the back, but there were more buttons than usual. The controls were unfamiliar to Jake. "I can't even tell which of these buttons is supposed to turn it on."

But as Jake tried pressing different buttons, the screen suddenly activated. "Okay," he said, "let's see if it works."

Lydia stood in front of the desk. Jake aimed the camera at her and took a picture. However, when he pressed what looked like the display button, a different image appeared on the screen. It was not Lydia. Eleanor was standing where Lydia should have been, working at her desk.

"That's weird," he murmured.

"What's up?" asked Lydia.

"It's a picture of your mom. It must have been stored in here. I wonder why I can't see the one I took of you? Hang on, I'll try again."

Jake took two more pictures. Again, when he accessed the photo review, the pictures showed Eleanor. But they were different pictures this time.

"Well, it's old," said Lydia, taking the camera and studying her mother's photo. "It probably hasn't been used in years."

"I guess. I thought I took your picture, but it probably didn't save." He paused. "I wonder if it takes videos."

Lydia tried out a few of the buttons and managed to find the video function.

"Yeah," she said as she pointed the camera at Jake. "Stand over by the desk, and I'll try it out."

"Should I say anything?"

"Whatever," Lydia said as she began filming.

When Lydia played back the video, the screen once again showed Eleanor, this time where Jake had been standing. She was holding a camera and appeared to be taking a picture of a coffee mug that sat on top of the desk. There was a flash and then, to Lydia's astonishment, the mug vanished.

She gasped.

"What is it?" asked Jake.

"Quiet," Lydia said, "she's saying something."

On the screen, Eleanor was speaking into a tape recorder.

> *"It looks like the experiment was a success. The mug travelled in time, just like all the other objects. Now it's time for the live animal trials, but not here. I need to continue the tests at the lab and should be able to work in peace tomorrow evening. Then, if all goes well, I'll do the human trial . . ."*

The video stopped abruptly and the screen went blank.

"What happened?" Lydia asked, pressing all the camera's buttons in a vain attempt to get it working again. "Is it the battery?"

"Let me take a look."

Lydia handed him the camera and Jake found a compartment that held a small battery.

"Do you have any of this type here?" he asked.

"Maybe. I can check upstairs."

"Don't worry. I probably have something back at home that will fit this."

They both heard the front door open as Greg returned. Jake placed the camera on the desk and followed Lydia up the basement steps.

"Hey, Dad," said Lydia as she walked into the kitchen. "You'll never guess what we found in Mom's old office."

"Not right now, Lydia," Greg said as he hurriedly emptied grocery bags, putting some things into the fridge and grabbing some plates from the kitchen cabinets. "Your Uncle Magnus called me just now from his cell. He'll be here in a few minutes. I assume you're staying for lunch, Jake?"

"Sure," Jake replied. "Thanks."

"Good," said Greg. "So can you two help me set the patio table?"

Lydia and Jake nodded.

"Thanks."

Chapter Two

Uncle Magnus

"So who's Uncle Magnus?" Jake asked as he and Lydia went onto the patio to set the table for lunch.

"He's not really my uncle. He was my mom's partner at the lab," answered Lydia. "They were close friends and worked together for quite a while on lots of research projects. Magnus was at the lab when Mom died. He tried to save her."

"Really?" said Jake.

"Yeah," Lydia said. "After the explosion, a huge fire broke out. Magnus nearly died going back in for my mom." She looked as if she was about to burst into tears.

The doorbell rang and they heard Greg greet Magnus. The men joined the two friends on the patio.

"This is Lydia's friend, Jake," Greg told Magnus.

Magnus shook Jake's hand, and Jake recognized him from the photograph he'd seen earlier, although Magnus' black hair was now flecked with grey and he had a deep scar on his left cheek beside his ear.

"Hi, Jake. How's it going?" asked Magnus.

"Fine, thanks," replied Jake.

"Okay," Greg said, "let's have some lunch, shall we? I'll get the drinks."

Lydia and Jake sat down at the table in the warm summer sunshine and Magnus took a seat opposite them.

"Lydia," said Magnus, "you're looking more like your beautiful mother every day."

"Thank you;" Lydia replied, with a bashful smile.

"It still seems strange, even after all this time, not working with her anymore," said Magnus with a sigh.

"You've done pretty well on your own though, Magnus," said Greg, returning with some lemonade and glasses.

"I suppose so. Sinclair Enterprises is doing pretty well."

"Pretty well?" He turned to Jake. "Magnus' company owns a huge tower downtown, and they have other offices all over the world. His company's invented so many new things, I've lost count."

"Do you have anything new coming up?" Lydia asked.

"Not right now," replied Magnus, shaking his head. "We're still dealing with the marketing of our latest medical imaging equipment. It's been a lot more work than we expected, to be honest."

"I don't pretend to understand it, or any other of your inventions," said Greg, "but it's uncanny how you've always beaten your rivals to the punch. Sometimes it seems to me that some company or other had been working on the same device, but you got there first. It's almost like you can see into the future."

Magnus looked a little uncomfortable. "Yes, it might seem like that, but there's an element of luck in it. I have extremely talented and dedicated people at Sinclair. Much of the credit really goes to them. I owe a lot to Eleanor as well."

"Thanks, Magnus," said Greg. "Lydia and I both appreciate how you've always helped preserve her memory and how you've remained a part of the family."

"We worked on some great things together," Magnus continued. "Really groundbreaking stuff, especially the projects related to photography. I've always wondered what might have become of those. I don't suppose you've come across any of Eleanor's research notes since the last time we talked?"

Greg laughed. "Not that again," he said. "I've told you before, Magnus, there was nothing here. I went through her home office after she died, and there was nothing. All Eleanor did was catch up on correspondence when she worked at home. You know how much she valued quality time with Lydia."

"Of course," Magnus said apologetically, smiling at Lydia.

For the remainder of the meal, Greg and Magnus discussed sports, politics, the stock market and the economy. They asked Lydia and Jake about their plans for the summer and about school. It was almost two o'clock when the meal finally drew to a close.

"Well, I have to get going," said Magnus as he stood up. "I have golf at three. It was great to catch up. Nice meeting you, Jake. Oh, I almost forgot—I gave Lydia one of these the last time I was here, so you may as well have one too."

He reached into his pocket and handed Jake a memory stick with the Sinclair Enterprises logo on the side. Next to it was a seal that read CHAMBER OF COMMERCE AWARD FOR OUTSTANDING ACHIEVEMENT, with the previous year's date printed in small letters underneath.

"We had those made up when we won the prize," Magnus explained. "You could use it for school."

"Sure," replied Jake, pocketing the memory stick. "Thanks a lot."

"Okay, well thank you for lunch, Greg, Lydia," said Magnus.

"Hey, any time, Magnus," Greg told him as he stood up. "You're always welcome. How's the Hummer?"

"Great," Magnus replied. "Want to check it out?"

"You bet," said Greg. He turned to Lydia. "You and Jake clear the table. I won't be long."

"No problem, Dad," Lydia told him. "Bye, Uncle Magnus."

"Bye, Lydia. Bye, Jake."

Lydia and Jake had almost finished clearing the table when Jake got a call on his cell.

"That was my mom," he told Lydia, hanging up. "I have to get home. I have a dentist appointment later this afternoon."

"Okay," said Lydia.

"Hey," Jake said, "can I take that camera home and see if I can get it working?"

"Sure," said Lydia. "I'll get it."

Chapter Three

Intruders

A week later, Lydia went over to Jake's house with her laptop. She had managed to find the charger, and although the computer had a few glitches, it worked well enough for Lydia and Jake to watch movies and play games on it with their friends Megan, Kyle and Jason.

Jake's place had become something of an unofficial headquarters for the school friends during . summer vacation. Ever since she'd known Jake and his family, Lydia had always been amazed at the contrast between his house and her own. Lydia's father was very organized. The house and garden were impeccably tidy. Jake's place, on the other hand, was a veritable

Aladdin's cave of mechanical equipment. Jake's dad liked to tinker with machinery, so the house was crowded with old radios and televisions. In the garage were heaps of old engines and rusty cans filled to the brim with screws, washers, nuts and bolts.

Jake had inherited his dad's curiosity about how things worked, but was more interested in electronics, cameras and computers. Just like his dad had his garage, Jake had a shed at the back of the house where he kept all his stuff.

He hadn't had any luck yet with the camera they'd found in Eleanor's basement office, but he promised Lydia that he would unlock the camera's secrets.

It was close to five thirty when Lydia headed home, but to her surprise as she rounded the corner at the end of her street, there were two police cruisers parked outside her home. Fearing the worst, Lydia held tightly on to the laptop and raced down the sidewalk until she reached the house. She sprinted up the driveway and past the police officer standing in the doorway talking to Greg.

"Dad, what is it?" she exclaimed. "What happened?"

"It's okay," Greg said. "We had a break-in while I was at work."

"Oh my God. Are you okay?"

"Yes," Greg replied. "The police think it happened sometime this afternoon, although it's tough to tell."

The big screen TV her dad had bought last Christmas was gone, along with the DVD player. Several framed photographs had been swept from the shelf over the fireplace, and there was broken glass all over the carpet. The drawers of the tall wooden cabinet were all open, and some of the kitchen drawers were open as well.

"There's some stuff missing from upstairs. Nothing from your room, but I guess you had your laptop with you?"

Lydia nodded.

"Whoever broke in took some of the electronic equipment from your mom's old office. Made quite a mess down there. They took some of her old jewellery too. Things I was hoping to give to you."

"Well, at least no one was hurt," said the police officer. "If you'd been home when they actually broke in, it might have been a very different story."

"True," Greg said. "I guess you're right, but still . . ."

"We'll be on our way once the guys get what prints they can from the furniture and doorways. There have been a few break-ins nearby over the last few weeks. These gangs usually concentrate on a particular neighbourhood, then move on."

"Do you think you'll catch them?" asked Lydia.

"We hope so," the officer said, smiling.

"Don't worry, Lydia," said Greg. "We have insurance, and I'll make sure everything's replaced."

Lydia smiled. But she was quite unnerved at the thought of strangers going through all their possessions, and knew she'd have trouble getting to sleep that night.

Chapter Four

Pictures of the Past

Jake's shed in the backyard was crammed with bits and pieces of modern machinery. The shelves and floor were littered with computers, monitors and laptops in various stages of assembly, countless cameras, cellphones and other hand-held electronic devices, some VCRs and DVD players, along with a couple of small televisions, all of which he intended to either fix, take apart or put back together. But instead Jake fiddled with the camera Lydia had given him to take home. He had managed to get it working again.

Jake stood inside the doorway and took a few photographs of the interior of the shed. However, when he checked to see if the pictures had been saved, instead of a shot of his cluttered workshop, Jake was shocked to see something completely different. In the photographs, the shed was filled with gardening equipment, including a hedge trimmer, lawn mower, two rakes hanging on wall hooks, and what looked like a small chainsaw. He zoomed in to see shelves stacked neatly with boxes of fertilizer and weed killer.

Jake realized that the shed looked exactly like it did when his family had first moved in, before he had cleared out all the garden tools and filled it with his own things. But that was a year ago. Why had Eleanor taken a photo of the previous owner's shed? And he wondered why the photos he had just taken were not showing up in the camera's memory.

Jake adjusted a few of the camera's controls and turned a knob beside the screen. He took four new pictures of the inside of his workshop.

When he checked the images, they showed himself, Lydia, Kyle, Jason and Megan watching movies on Lydia's laptop, as they had been doing two days before.

Jake grabbed his cell from his worktable and called Lydia.

"Hey, it's me," he said. "Get over here right away."

"Why?" asked Lydia. "What's up?"

"I got the camera working again," Jake told her, "but there's something you need to see."

"What is it?"

"You have to see for yourself."

"Okay," said Lydia. "I'll come right over."

"Bring the laptop."

"Sure. Be there soon."

A short time later, Lydia entered the shed.

"So what's up?" she asked Jake as she placed the laptop on one of the wooden chairs.

"Like I said," Jake explained, "I got the camera working, but there's definitely something weird going on."

"Such as?" prompted Lydia.

"Well," Jake began, holding up the camera, "once I got this to start up, I took some pictures. But the same thing happened as last time. The pictures didn't save, but I saw some other photos."

"Like the one of Mom that's stored in the camera?"

"Not exactly. It was a picture of what this shed looked like before we moved in."

He handed her the camera and Lydia studied the picture of the shed filled with gardening equipment.

"I don't get it," she said.

"Now look at the other pictures," said Jake, showing her which button to press. "I took them after adjusting that knob to the left of the screen."

Lydia scrolled through the other photographs, seeing herself and her friends in the shed.

"But nobody took any pictures that day," she said. "You didn't even have the camera working then."

"Exactly," said Jake. "This camera takes pictures of the past."

"That's impossible!"

"Turning that knob makes the camera take pictures of a different time!"

"That must have been what my mom was working on late into the night. Let me try."

"Sure. It's still set to when everyone was over here."

Lydia turned the knob slightly and took two pictures. They showed her coming through the doorway of the shed, as she had a few moments earlier.

"Incredible."

"We might be able to upload the pictures onto the laptop so we can see them better," said Jake.

Lydia handed him the camera and Jake cleared some space on his worktable. He connected the camera to the USB port.

"I wonder if there's anything stored on the laptop about your mom's project," Jake said as the pictures uploaded.

Jake soon found some videos and opened one that showed scenes in the laboratory at Chamberlain Research.

In one video, Eleanor was standing before the camera and speaking.

"Our work began with a mutual interest in photography. We were surprised at how closely our interests converged. Both Magnus and I believed that reflected light stayed on objects such as brick walls, houses and other solid structures, and we thought that if we could capture that light, it could develop into a kind of time photography. We did research for many years, until we finally succeeded in making a specially adapted camera. We were able to capture images of people and objects that were not present when we took the photographs. Impossible as it seemed, we initially thought we had taken pictures of ghosts. However, we soon realized that we'd actually captured images from the past. The images appeared to predate the invention of photography. We took the camera to Europe to see how far back into the past we could photograph."

At that point the video stopped, giving Jake and Lydia some time to reflect on what they'd just witnessed.

"Can you believe that?" said Jake.

But Lydia was crying.

"I'm sorry," Jake said. "I shouldn't have put you through this."

"It's okay," she said, catching her breath. "It's actually nice to see my mom. Makes her seem closer somehow. Let's see the rest."

"Well, if you're sure . . ." Jake said.

"I'm sure."

Jake opened up a folder containing some photographs taken in Paris. They were modern snapshots from the French Revolution, showing aristocrats in powdered wigs and a baying mob.

"Could they be fakes?" asked Lydia.

"Don't think so. Look at the clothes, the horses, the carriages and everything else. These are pictures from the eighteenth century. Those buildings in France have been there for hundreds of years, but these photos look like they were taken yesterday. Amazing."

"It's crazy, isn't it? But it seems to be real."

"It looks that way. I think you can set the camera to show a specific moment in time at a particular place."

"Because of the light staying in one place or something? Wasn't that what my mom said?"

"Exactly."

"So that film of Mom in the basement office wasn't a recording. It was actually the past."

"That's what I'm thinking. But hang on, there's another video here."

Chapter Five

A Dangerous Discovery

Jake clicked on the icon and the file opened. Eleanor and Magnus appeared on the screen. Magnus spoke first.

> *"The further we went back in time, the more distorted the images became."*

> *"So, we did more work, but we also decided that we wouldn't publish our findings until we were absolutely sure. After all, if we could take pictures of the past, perhaps we could also take*

pictures of the future. We haven't tested that particular theory yet, but we're both convinced that we can adapt the camera somehow to capture images of the future. However . . ."

At that point, the video abruptly stopped.

"Is that all?" asked Lydia.

"Looks like it," Jake replied.

"It's incredible that they could take pictures of the past," Lydia said. "Do you really think they could take pictures of the future as well?"

"No idea." Jake shrugged. "That's all we've got. Unless . . ."

He began typing something on the keyboard.

"What is it?" Lydia asked him.

"There are some password-protected files here," Jake explained. "They might be nothing. But they could have more details about the project."

"Can you open them?" asked Lydia.

"Done," Jake replied."Easy to crack."

The hidden files contained detailed notes about the camera that they'd found in the basement and some more pictures.

"Nothing new then," said Lydia.

"No," Jake agreed, "just more of your mom's research with Magnus."

He was about to close the computer when he noticed something that seemed oddly out of place. "Just a second," he murmured.

"What?"

"I'm not sure," said Jake. The photograph showed a page of newspaper. Jake zoomed closer on the picture. "Look at the date! It's five years from now."

"How can you take pictures of something that hasn't happened yet? Could it be a hoax?"

"I guess. They could easily be fakes with all the technology we have these days. But your mom was a scientist."

"Wait a minute," said Lydia. "If you could use the camera to see the past here, why can't we use it in Mom's basement office? Maybe we can find out a bit more about those experiments she mentioned, you know, the one with that coffee mug and those animal tests."

"Good idea," Jake agreed. "Your dad's at work, right?"

"Yeah," replied Lydia, "we'll have plenty of time before he gets home."

Back at the Chamberlains' house in the basement office, Jake adjusted the time settings on the camera, pointed the device at Eleanor's desk and pressed the record button. After a few minutes, Jake stopped recording and then uploaded the video onto Lydia's laptop. Jake and Lydia watched as an image of Eleanor appeared. She was speaking into a voice recorder using a lapel microphone.

> "... *too important to fall into the wrong hands. I'm not even sure if there's anyone in the world capable of handling something like this. The camera has the power to take pictures of a different time, but is also capable of transporting objects into the past or even into the future.*"

Jake and Lydia turned to each other in amazement. They watched as Eleanor placed a mug on her desk. She seemed to be preparing for an experiment.

> *"The first version of the camera could take pictures through time, which was amazing enough. However, even though Magnus and I thought it might also be used to travel through time, or at least to send objects back and forth, I decided to explore that possibility myself. I'm using an enhanced version of the camera on my own. That's why I'm testing it here at the house, rather than at Chamberlain Research."*

"Wonder why she didn't do this at the lab?" Lydia pondered.

"Yeah, that's kind of weird," agreed Jake. "Maybe she'll tell us later."

They both watched as Eleanor pointed the camera at the mug.

> *"I'll take a picture of the mug after changing the time-travel settings to one hour into the past. If my theory's correct the mug should disappear."*

Jake and Lydia observed as Eleanor took a picture of the mug, which instantly vanished. She continued talking as the camera remained focused on the top of the desk.

> *"In addition to the time-travel function, this camera can also take pictures of the past, like the earlier model. So if I take a photo of how my desk looked one hour ago, I should see the mug there, even though it wasn't there before."*

Eleanor adjusted the settings on the camera and took a photograph of her desk.

> *"Yes! It really works! The mug travelled one hour into the past."*

She abruptly stopped speaking when, out of nowhere, the mug reappeared. Tentatively, she picked it up off the desk.

> "It seems that the object will return to its own time after a few minutes. Perhaps it's possible to increase the amount of time that the object stays in the past."

The recording showed Eleanor making some notes on her laptop about what she'd observed, and then it ended.

Jake and Lydia recorded several more videos and watched the rest of her experiments in the basement office. Eleanor sent other objects into the past, each one for increasingly longer periods, before retrieving them.

> "It looks like the experiment was a success. The mug travelled in time, just like all the other objects. Now it's time for the live animal trials, but not here. I need to continue the tests at the lab

and should be able to work in peace
tomorrow evening. Then, if all goes well,
I'll do the human trial and use myself as
the first subject."

Eleanor then exited the basement office, leaving the screen empty.

"Where were you when this was happening?" Jake asked.

"My grandparents' house," replied Lydia. "Mom sent me and Dad away for a few days. I thought she just wanted us to have a nice holiday. Obviously she wanted the house to herself so she could do all these tests in secret."

"Well, if we want to see what happened with those animal tests, we need to take the camera over to the Chamberlain Research lab, or where the lab used to be. It's too late now. We'll have to go there tomorrow." Jake pondered for a moment. "I think what we have here is the enhanced camera, the one with the time-travel function, since that's the one your mom kept at home. I wonder what happened to the other model?"

Chapter Six

Sinclair Enterprises

On the uppermost floor of the Sinclair Enterprises tower in the heart of downtown, Magnus Sinclair gazed out of his office window at the city streets far below as the last of the rush hour traffic thinned out. He often worked late.

He turned away from the window and looked around the room, glancing at the awards he'd received from around the world for his inventions and breakthroughs in science and technology. The walls were adorned with pictures of him with celebrities, royalty, prime ministers and presidents. It had been a very busy couple of years. Magnus Sinclair had become a multimillionaire, with global commercial interests in medicine and hi-tech industries. As he settled back in his office chair, Magnus reflected on how it all began.

He'd worked with Eleanor for almost a decade at Chamberlain Research and they'd become friends as well as colleagues. Magnus had acted as godfather when Eleanor's daughter was born and had become a close friend of the family.

He and Eleanor had worked on a number of projects together, but those related to light and photography had been the most important. Each had agreed to not release their findings until they were absolutely sure about how the technology worked. However, they hadn't been in agreement about everything. As Magnus repeatedly pointed out to Eleanor, the ability to take pictures of the future could make them both wealthy beyond their wildest dreams. Yet despite the fact that they'd tested the camera and even taken pictures of future news headlines, Eleanor was firmly opposed to any further development in that area. They'd had furious arguments about it, but Magnus never thought Eleanor would go so far as to destroy all their years of hard work.

He'd almost been too late when he'd surprised her at the lab as she was burning their research materials. But he'd saved the camera itself and made good use of it since Eleanor's death. They hadn't been able to view scenes more than a few years into the future without the images breaking up, but Magnus hadn't needed to perfect the technology. After all, it wasn't that necessary for him to see the upcoming centuries. Just a year or so would suffice for Magnus' schemes to succeed. By taking pictures of events to come, Magnus had anticipated share prices on the stock market, making a huge fortune. He also gambled on horse races, but always remained careful not to win too much and attract unwelcome attention.

Soon, however, it was not enough to just make money. Magnus craved fame as well. He had always wanted to be known for an important scientific breakthrough, and now that revealing the time camera to the world was out of the question, Magnus began to use it to steal inventions and patents from other researchers. New technological breakthroughs were always kept under wraps and jealously guarded from the competition until they were ready to be launched. Magnus was able to use the camera to steal his competitors' ideas before they were made public. He would then develop the technology himself, together with the teams of experts he could now afford to hire with the immense wealth he'd managed to acquire. Although his business rivals were envious and somewhat resentful of Magnus' success, they considered his knack of anticipating market trends uncanny, but not suspicious. Sinclair Enterprises rapidly grew into a huge multinational corporation, and Magnus had everything anyone could want, and more.

And yet, despite his success, he often thought about the time-travel aspects of the technology that they had abandoned. He sometimes considered the possibility that Eleanor might have worked on the time-travel theory alone. Magnus had arranged the burglary at their home to see if he could find anything that had been hidden. However, his men had found nothing at the Chamberlains' house, and Magnus had finally accepted that Eleanor hadn't been working on anything else after all.

But the lure of the future was irresistible. Magnus walked over to a large portrait of himself. He gently eased the gilded frame away from the wall and it swung open, revealing the concealed safe and adjacent keypad. Magnus entered a numerical code and opened the door. The safe contained a solitary item, a perfectly ordinary-looking black digital camera. He smiled as he locked the safe, closed the portrait frame and returned to his desk with the camera.

Magnus sat down in front of his computer and activated the camera. He used it to study a future online article about a new medical diagnostic device that a rival company was working on. He had been following the device's development for some time and determined that it had now reached the stage in the present when he could steal the technology for himself. Magnus read the financial news from two years into the future. Sure enough, the company's value had skyrocketed since the invention had gone on the market.

He had already made arrangements to gain access to the company's research department so that he could take pictures of all the relevant blueprints and project files. Crucially, he would need pictures of the device itself, even though it had not yet been built. Since that required the use of the time camera, he could trust no one else to carry out the mission. Magnus turned off the computer and quickly left the office.

It didn't take Magnus long to reach the research facility, located on the outskirts of the downtown core. He had informants working for most of his competitors, who from time to time supplied him with confidential material about new technological breakthroughs. Sometimes this information was of little interest, but the diagnostic device was destined to make millions in the future, and Magnus was determined that the machine be developed by Sinclair Enterprises. His contact this time was a security guard, who had been well paid for his betrayal.

Magnus pulled into the parking lot and drove

around to the rear of the building, where the security guard was waiting for him at the delivery door.

"Did you get the money?" asked Magnus as he approached.

"Yeah, last night," said the guard.

"Good. So where's the lab?"

"Just through here," replied the guard, holding the door slightly ajar, "but I can't give you a lot of time in there."

"Don't worry," Magnus assured him, "I won't be long."

The guard had arranged for the security system to be temporarily disabled while Magnus was inside. Magnus soon reached the main lab. Naturally the blueprints and design specifications had been placed in a secure location for the night. However, Magnus took out the camera and was able to peer a couple of days into the future. He found a point in time when the company's research scientists were working on the project, and took pictures of their blueprints and files. Magnus then adjusted the camera's settings so he could photograph several months into the future. He took pictures of the completed device before hurrying back to the exit.

"So when will you send the rest of the money?" the guard asked when Magnus emerged from the facility.

"My people will contact you tomorrow," said Magnus as he walked over to his car. But he was not about to risk everything by leaving the guard as a witness to his crime. After driving away, he placed a call on his cell.

"It's done," Magnus said. "The guard will be there for a while. You know what to do."

Chapter Seven

Stealing Tomorrow

The next day, Jake and Lydia made the short bus trip from Lydia's house to the site of Chamberlain Research. There wasn't much left of the original structure, just the short remnants of a couple of walls and the outlines of the building's foundations. The lot still stood empty and prominently displayed a FOR SALE sign next to the sidewalk.

"Is this going to work?" asked Lydia. "There's nothing here anymore."

"It should work," Jake told her. "The camera should be able to take pictures of how the lab looked in the past. Let's give it a try."

Since neither of them were familiar with the

layout of the Chamberlain Research building, Jake pointed the camera at a few different places and took pictures until he managed to find the spot where Eleanor had conducted her experiments. He then shot several short videos, adjusting the time settings slightly before each recording.

The first couple of videos they watched showed nothing of interest, but then they saw Eleanor standing in the main laboratory. Behind her were four individual cages, one containing mice, another a couple of rats.

> "... tests have now all been completed, and there appear to have been no problems. I've conducted a full examination of each animal that has been transported and all are in perfect health, showing no signs of deterioration. There does, however, seem to be a limit as to how long an object can remain in the past. When this limit expires, the object will snap back to its own time without warning. This is clearly something I need to investigate further,

> *but the next step will be to conduct the first tests on humans, namely myself, tomorrow morning back at home."*

The screen went blank. Jake accessed the next video and hit play. This time both Eleanor and Magnus appeared on the screen, engaged in a heated discussion. Magnus spoke first.

> *"Look, Eleanor, all I'm saying is that we shouldn't be so hasty. Think of the incredible possibilities of being able to see into the future."*

> *"To do what? I agree it has potential, but someone will always be tempted to use the technology for their own gain."*

> *"You think someone might use it to bet on horse races and the stock market?"*

> *"Most definitely, Magnus!"*

"But what about actually sending objects, or even people, into the past or the future? We should really investigate that."

"I'm really not sure that's a good idea. It's something that should be left alone."

"What! After all the time we've spent on this?"

"It's too dangerous, Magnus!"

"After all we've been through together?"

"It isn't that. Someone would always be tempted to make themself rich—make themselves powerful. You know exactly what I mean."

"So, Eleanor, what do we do with all our research?"

"We have to abandon the project. I can't in all good conscience allow our discovery to reach the public."

"After all our work, I still can't believe you'd throw it all away."

"I know we've worked hard, Magnus, but I've made my decision."

"But, Eleanor . . ."

"There's nothing more to discuss. Goodnight."

The small screen showed Magnus turn on his heel and storm out of the laboratory. Jake and Lydia watched as Eleanor dropped into a chair, her brow deeply furrowed with anxiety.

"Well," Jake said, "it looks like Magnus and your mom had very different ideas about the camera. I'll bet he planned on stealing it for himself."

"I can't believe he'd ever betray my mom."

"But the camera had the power to view the future," Jake pointed out, "and you can't deny he's become very wealthy since your mom died."

"That's crazy," said Lydia. "They were friends. Magnus would never do anything like that."

"But remember your dad saying how uncanny it was that Magnus seemed able to predict the future?"

"Dad just meant in terms of his business, getting a jump on the competition, that sort of thing."

"Not so uncanny if you can see into the future with this camera, is it?"

Lydia didn't answer. "Let's get back to the house," she finally said without emotion. "We'll be able see if she actually carried out those tests."

"Wait," said Jake. "Let's just watch one more video."

He pressed play, and on the screen they were both shocked to see that the entire laboratory was on fire. It looked as if there'd been an explosion. In the debris, Eleanor was trapped beneath a heavy steel filing cabinet.

"Magnus! Magnus! Help me, I can't move my legs!"

Magnus must have been there somewhere in the devastated laboratory. Yet as Jake and Lydia looked on in horror, he failed to come to Eleanor's aid.

"Magnus! Don't leave me!"

"Oh my God," Lydia gasped.

Jake was eager to see what happened next, but Lydia reached over and switched off the camera, looking shaken.

"What's the matter?" Jake asked her.

"If there is any more video," Lydia replied, "the next thing we'll see is my mom's death."

Chapter Eight

Future Imperfect

Back at his office, Magnus studied the pictures he had taken the night before. He'd get his staff to work on the blueprints right away, and Sinclair Enterprises would soon have a version of the diagnostic machine on the market. Magnus smiled to himself.

Using the time camera once again, he was surprised when, instead of a view of future online news headlines, all he saw was an empty desk. His computer was missing. The three-tier in-tray was also gone, along with the collection of papers and folders. At first Magnus merely suspected a camera malfunction, but grew more alarmed as he took other pictures around the office. All the filing cabinets had been removed and, most disturbing of all, the portrait frame was pulled away from the wall and the concealed safe was open. This was no malfunction. The camera was working perfectly and was showing him a less than perfect future. Magnus then remembered the news kiosk in the adjacent building beside the coffee shop. He shoved the camera into his jacket pocket, grabbed his keys and hurried out of the office, completely ignoring his secretary's inquiries as he hurried to the elevator.

Standing in front of the news kiosk, Magnus aimed the camera at the newspapers on display and took some photos. On the camera's screen, in the newspaper headline, he saw his own name and that of his company. The article was about the company being wound up amid allegations of corrupt business practices.

Magnus stepped away from the kiosk and went to sit in the nearby coffee shop to study the pictures in more detail. On closer examination, he was shocked at what he read. It reported that Magnus himself had been placed under arrest for fraud, stock market manipulation and insider trading. There seemed to be ample evidence of Magnus' guilt. But there was no mention of the camera. He wondered how on earth he'd been discovered. Further down in the article, he noted a reference to the Chamberlain family in connection with his work with Eleanor at Chamberlain Research. It appeared that Lydia and her friend had something to do with his future arrest. There were no other details, and Magnus switched off the camera in alarm.

Eleanor must have made another camera, Magnus thought. *How else could those kids know what I've done? Lydia and Jake must have the other camera that Eleanor secretly worked on. I'll have to do something about those kids.*

He took out his phone and dialed a number.

"Meet me over at the Chamberlain house," he said. "Yes, the one with the basement office. I'll join you in thirty minutes."

Chapter Nine

An Unwelcome Visitor

"What are we going to do?" asked Lydia.

"We have to tell your dad," Jake told her. "He'll know what to do. It'll look crazy if a couple of kids go to the police with a story like this. Who's going to believe us? Will your dad be back from work yet?"

"Not sure," said Lydia. "He works late sometimes. And I never know when to expect him. He usually gives me a call."

"Okay, let's get over to your place."

At the Chamberlain house, Magnus was in the basement. Two men were tying Greg down onto the office chair. Greg had a trickle of blood running from the corner of his mouth, and the beginnings of a black eye. The home office had been torn apart. The door to the secret compartment was open. The hiding space was empty except for a lens cover.

"Magnus," Greg pleaded, "I don't understand. What's all this about?"

"So you still refuse to talk?" asked Magnus with a snarl, ignoring the question.

"Magnus, I've told you before, I don't know anything about any secret work Eleanor was doing. You know I had nothing to do with all that."

"But Lydia does," said Magnus, "and so does her friend, Jake."

"What are you talking about? You're not making any sense."

"You see, Greg," Magnus explained, "Eleanor and I made an amazing discovery. It involved being able to take photographs of the past and future. But Eleanor worried that someone might want to use the technology for their own gain."

"You mean . . ."

"That's right," Magnus said, interrupting him. "I wanted to use the device to make us rich. Eleanor disagreed and wanted to abandon the entire project. The explosion at the lab was an accident, and I could have saved her, Greg, but I decided not to. I had the camera all to myself."

"So you let my wife die!"

"Yes," Magnus said. "And I used the camera to steal other people's work, but as I always suspected, Eleanor had developed another device on her own. She must have hidden it here," he said, pointing at the hiding place. "But it isn't here, is it? Lydia and her friend must have it."

"Lydia and Jake? Why do you think they have it?"

"Because, Greg, I've seen the future. They go to the police with what they've discovered. Those kids hold my fate in their hands. Now where are they?"

"I don't know, Magnus, I swear. I've been at work all day. I honestly have no idea."

"Enough!" barked Magnus, slapping Greg hard across the face with the back of his hand. "You're no use to me at all. And now you know too much."

He strode toward the basement steps, then turned to face his men.

"Burn everything," he snapped, "and make sure he doesn't leave here alive."

The men nodded as Magnus stormed out of the basement.

By the time Jake and Lydia reached the house, the flames were already beginning to spew out the front door. Magnus' Hummer was parked in the driveway next to Greg's car. Another car was parked on the street.

"Dad!" exclaimed Lydia.

She started toward the house, but Jake held her back.

"You'll die in there!" Jake exclaimed. "I'll call the fire department."

He took out his phone, but before he could dial the number, Magnus came around the side of the house.

"Leave that guy and come out here," he shouted over his shoulder.

Two thuggish men lumbered up to Magnus and stared across the driveway at Lydia and Jake.

"Get them!" Magnus ordered, pointing.

"Run!" yelled Jake.

"But my dad's in there!"

"There's no time to save him! Run!"

Jake and Lydia sprinted away from the house with Magnus' men in pursuit. As they approached the neighbourhood convenience store, Jake slowed down and pointed over at a large dumpster.

"Over there," he said.

But before they could slip behind the dumpster they heard a shout.

"There they are!"

Lydia and Jake raced into the adjacent alley, only to be confronted with a nine-foot-high chain-link fence, which they struggled to scale. When they finally did drop to the other side, Magnus' men had closed in.

Thinking fast, Lydia took the camera from her pocket, quickly changed its settings and took a picture of Jake and herself.

One of Magnus' men landed right beside her and snatched the camera from Lydia's grasp, just as the flash went off and Lydia and Jake vanished.

Chapter Ten

Journey to Yesterday

Lydia and Jake were still in the alley beside the fence, but there was no sign of the men who'd been chasing them.

"Jake, are you okay?" Lydia asked.

"I think so," he answered.

There was something different about their surroundings. All the trees had yellow leaves or bare branches, whereas before they had been lush and green.

"What's going on?" Jake asked.

"It worked."

"What do you mean?"

"The camera. I think we've gone back in time to the day my mom died."

"Are you sure?" asked Jake in disbelief. "How can you tell?"

"I set the date on the camera to the day she died and then took our picture. The explosion was in October. Look around. It was summer when we left, and it's fall now."

"Incredible."

"We need to find out for sure. Come on."

The two of them went into a nearby convenience store and looked at a newspaper. It was dated October 1, two years earlier.

The cashier eyed them suspiciously.

"We need to hurry," said Lydia, looking at her watch and hustling Jake outside.

"What's the rush?" Jake asked as they stood on the sidewalk.

"It's ten o'clock. The explosion won't happen for another hour. If we move fast, we can save my mom," Lydia said.

"What about your dad?" asked Jake.

"When I set the time on the camera, I thought about going back far enough to try to save my dad, and then I figured maybe we could go back further and save them both."

"Where *is* the camera?" Jake asked.

"One of those guys who were after us grabbed it out of my hand right when it flashed. They must still have it."

"This is bad. This is really bad."

"Don't forget, we don't have that long before we snap back to our own time."

"Exactly how long do we have?"

"No clue. My mom didn't say."

"Okay, let's get moving."

Jake and Lydia took a cab to Chamberlain Research. A familiar vehicle stopped outside the building as their cab pulled into the parking lot. It was Greg's car, with Lydia in the passenger seat.

"That's me, isn't it?"

"Yes," said Jake. "Stay out of sight. I think you should avoid meeting yourself."

Jake watched as Eleanor got out of the car.

She gave Greg a kiss on the cheek before they exchanged a few words and the car drove away. Clutching her briefcase, Eleanor hurried to the front entrance of Chamberlain Research and went inside.

"So how are we going to explain our presence here to my mom?" asked Lydia.

"I have no idea, but we don't really have a choice. Let's hope she's pretty open to the idea of time travellers. After all, she invented the camera, didn't she? Now let's go."

Chapter Eleven

A Change of Course

Lydia and Jake entered the laboratory. Eleanor was tossing papers into the wastebasket. Then she held up a camera, looking like she was going to drop that in as well.

"Hi, Mom," said Lydia, her voice breaking. Lydia couldn't help staring at her mother, whom she'd been mourning for nearly two years.

"Hi, Lydia," said Eleanor in surprise. "What are you doing here? You look upset. And . . . different. And who are you?" she asked, turning to Jake.

"My name is Jake," he said. "Lydia and I are

from the future. We travelled here to warn you about Magnus Sinclair."

"What are you talking about? From the future?"

"We used your time camera," said Lydia. "Jake is my friend in the future. Mom, you're in terrible danger. You have to believe me. We don't have much time."

"What do you mean?" asked Eleanor.

"You have to believe us," Lydia told her. "Magnus will come here, and there's going to be a fire."

Jake and Lydia told Eleanor everything that had happened since they'd discovered the camera.

Jake dug into his pocket and pulled out the memory stick Magnus had given him after lunch on the patio. "Here," he said as he handed it over to Eleanor.

She examined the logos of Sinclair Enterprises and the Chamber of Commerce. "Sinclair Enterprises!" she exclaimed.

"Magnus gave it to me. He had it made after winning an award for one of the many inventions he's stolen," said Jake.

"Sinclair Enterprises is a huge corporation in the future," Lydia added. "Magnus uses the camera to find out about new inventions his business rivals are developing just as they're about to come on the market, then claims them as his own."

"He suggested that to me," Eleanor said. "That's why I want to destroy everything."

"You're standing in his way," said Jake, "but . . ."

"There's going to be a fire here at the lab," said Lydia, "and you'll die."

"Die!" exclaimed Eleanor.

"Unless we change what happens," Jake said.

"And we can save Dad too," said Lydia.

They told Eleanor what had happened when the house had been set on fire, with Greg still inside.

"I never told your dad what I was working on—to protect him." Eleanor was silent for a moment. "I'm amazed that the time-travel technology actually works. I've never had the chance to test it on humans. There must be two versions of both of you in this time period."

"Yes," said Lydia. "Jake pointed that out just before we came in here. He said that we probably shouldn't run into each other."

"Good idea," said Eleanor. "So what do we do now?"

"Magnus will be here any minute," Jake said. "We need to get out of here before he arrives."

"Plus, we don't know how long we can stay in this time," Lydia added. "Because of the snap-back effect."

"You're right," said Eleanor. "Let's get out now."

But when they stepped into the corridor, they saw Magnus entering the building.

"Quick," Eleanor said, "hide here."

She shut the door. Jake and Lydia hid behind a tall filing cabinet while Eleanor set the wastepaper basket alight.

"What do you think you're doing?" Magnus asked, coming into the room.

Eleanor spun around to see her research partner, Magnus Sinclair, standing in the doorway less than twenty feet away.

"I already told you, Magnus," Eleanor replied, maintaining a firm grip on the camera, "this project is too dangerous."

"What are you talking about?" he asked, edging toward her.

"You know what I mean, Magnus," she said sternly. "You said as much yourself."

"But think of the possibilities, Eleanor! We could both be rich beyond our wildest dreams. You know as well as I do, this isn't about the past. It's about the future. About the technology and all the inventions still to be discovered. It could all belong to us."

"It's still theft, no matter how you look at it."

"But no one would ever know," Magnus retorted. "How could they?"

"I can't allow it," insisted Eleanor, shaking her head. "I already burned all the research notes and deleted all the computer files. We need to end this—right now."

But when she turned to drop the camera into the fire, Magnus lunged at her. At the same time, Jake and Lydia pushed the heavy metal cabinet over on top of him, knocking him unconscious and pinning him to the floor next to the burning metal wastepaper basket.

Suddenly, someone appeared out of thin air.

Chapter Twelve

Twisting Time

"Nobody move," Magnus Sinclair ordered, pointing a gun at them. "Stay exactly where you are."

"Magnus!" Eleanor exclaimed.

"Oh, don't look so shocked, Eleanor," Magnus said. "You knew that time travel was possible, and you kept it from me."

"How did you get here?" Eleanor asked.

Magnus glanced at his unconscious younger self and held up the time-travel camera. "One of my men snatched it from the girl." He scowled at Lydia. "He told me how Lydia and Jake had vanished, and I realized what had happened. I'm here to make sure they don't succeed in changing the past. I've come here in order to save the future. Well . . . *my* future, really. You three, of course, are surplus to those plans."

He slipped the time-travel camera back into his jacket pocket.

"Now give me the other camera," he demanded. "I took it from you once before and need to ensure that history isn't changed. Hand it over."

"Mom, you can't!" exclaimed Lydia. "You can't let him have it!"

"I have no choice, Lydia," said Eleanor calmly. "He's the one with the gun."

"But he'll kill us anyway, no matter what you do," Jake said. "Don't give it to him!"

"I'm sorry, Jake," said Eleanor. "There's nothing I can do." She took three steps forward until she was standing just a few feet away from Magnus, and held out the camera in her open hand.

"A wise decision, Eleanor," said Magnus with a cruel smirk. "I was hoping you'd decide to see things my way." He reached out to take the camera from her.

Suddenly, Lydia, hoping to distract Magnus,

grabbed a jar of chemicals and threw the contents into the burning wastepaper basket. The fire flared up, and burning papers flew out and landed on the Magnus who was trapped under the filing cabinet. Momentarily forgetting about Eleanor, Jake and Lydia, the older Magnus rushed over to him and began beating out the flames.

"Come on!" urged Eleanor. "We have to get out of here!"

Eleanor, Lydia and Jake ran out of the laboratory and down the corridor to safety, as Magnus grabbed his gun and gave chase.

"Stop!" he shouted, firing his weapon down the corridor. Just then, however, an explosion erupted from the laboratory. Magnus glanced into what remained of the lab, realizing to his horror that he had to rescue his younger self, still trapped beneath the filing cabinet.

If I die in the fire, I'll cease to exist, he thought, hurrying back into the flames.

Eleanor lay prostrate on the tiled floor of the corridor, surrounded by shattered glass, with blood coming out of a wound in her shoulder and a deep gash across the back of her left hand.

"I've been shot! Get out of here fast!" she shouted at Jake and Lydia.

"But, Mom!" exclaimed Lydia.

"Go!" she yelled. "Save yourselves, there could be another explosion at any time! Run!"

"Jake!" Lydia exclaimed. "We can't just leave her!"

Jake moved toward Eleanor, but there was a massive explosion from the laboratory, and Jake and Lydia vanished.

Chapter Thirteen

Reversal of Fortunes

Jake and Lydia reappeared back in the alley near the convenience store. It was now early in the evening, and the colour of the leaves on the surrounding trees told them it was the height of summer. They'd been snapped back to their own time.

"We didn't help my dad, and we couldn't save my mom either," said Lydia, fighting back tears. "She's dead all over again and it's our fault."

"We don't actually know that," Jake said.

"Yes we do," sobbed Lydia. "She's dead. The

whole place exploded again just like the first time."

"She might still have made it," Jake said, doubtfully.

They raced through the neighbourhood streets until they reached Lydia's house. There was no sign of Magnus' Hummer, and Greg's car wasn't parked in the driveway. Surprisingly, the house showed no evidence of fire damage.

"Let's have a look inside," said Jake.

The front door wasn't locked, and Lydia entered the house first. From the hallway, she could see into the kitchen and noticed that the sliding door that led to the outdoor patio was open.

Jake gestured for her to follow him into the sitting room. He'd spotted the framed photographs on the shelf above the fireplace, and they both went over to examine them. To their astonishment, the family portraits were different. The pictures of Lydia with her dad now all had Eleanor in them as well.

"Mom must be alive!" said Lydia. "I wonder if she's here?"

"Look at this. Your mom has that gash on her hand."

In the photograph, Eleanor had a scar running across her left hand, extending from one side to the other.

Lydia stared open-mouthed in amazement at the photographs. "I wonder what happened to Magnus."

"Hey, check this out!" Jake said.

He held up a picture of Eleanor and Magnus in the laboratory, holding a brass plaque denoting some kind of an award, inscribed with the words CHAMBERLAIN RESEARCH and a date. However, an adhesive strip at the bottom of the frame read IN MEMORY OF MAGNUS SINCLAIR, followed by Magnus' date of birth and, more crucially, the date of his death two years earlier.

"So he died in the explosion instead of my mom," Lydia murmured. "This is so weird."

"There you are!"

Jake and Lydia both whirled around to see Eleanor standing there.

"Mom! You're alive!" exclaimed Lydia as she

rushed over to hug her mother.

"I certainly hope so," Eleanor replied. "Did something happen?"

"Oh, nothing," said Lydia. "What's for dinner? I'm starving."

"Your dad's bringing some things from the store," replied Eleanor, looking at Lydia through narrowed eyes. "I thought we'd sit out on the patio, since it's so nice out. Why don't you go outside and start getting some things ready?"

"Okay," said Lydia, leaving the sitting room.

"You're very welcome to stay and eat with us, Jake," said Eleanor, studying him closely. "You know, I just had the strangest feeling, that . . . are you okay?"

"Yeah," Jake replied, "I'm fine, thanks."

Eleanor shot him a curious glance. "You can help Lydia set the table."

Out on the patio, Lydia grabbed Jake's arm. "Magnus is dead, and Mom's alive!"

"But she doesn't remember what happened," Jake whispered.

"She must have lost her memory in the

explosion. It doesn't matter. I'm just glad to have her back."

Jake helped her set the table, as Lydia looked forward to a family meal she never thought she'd experience again.